Dear Parent:
Your child's love of reading starts here!

Every child learns to read in a different way and at his or her own speed. Some go back and forth between reading levels and read favorite books again and again. Others read through each level in order. You can help your young reader improve and become more confident by encouraging his or her own interests and abilities. From books your child reads with you to the first books he or she reads alone, there are I Can Read Books for every stage of reading:

SHARED READING
Basic language, word repetition, and whimsical illustrations, ideal for sharing with your emergent reader

BEGINNING READING
Short sentences, familiar words, and simple concepts for children eager to read on their own

READING WITH HELP
Engaging stories, longer sentences, and language play for developing readers

READING ALONE
Complex plots, challenging vocabulary, and high-interest topics for the independent reader

I Can Read Books have introduced children to the joy of reading since 1957. Featuring award-winning authors and illustrators and a fabulous cast of beloved characters, I Can Read Books set the standard for beginning readers.

A lifetime of discovery begins with the magical words **"I Can Read!"**

Visit www.icanread.com for information
on enriching your child's reading experience.

To every little ninja out there!
—N.D.W.

For Cousin Louie, the jolly volcano
—F.D.

I Can Read® and I Can Read Book® are trademarks of HarperCollins Publishers.

Hello, Ninja. Hello, Stage Fright!
Text copyright © 2021 by N. D. Wilson
Illustrations copyright © 2021 by Forrest Dickison
www.icanread.com

Library of Congress Control Number: 2021936195
ISBN 978-0-06-305621-3 (trade bdg.) — ISBN 978-0-06-305620-6 (pbk.)

Book design by Rachel Zegar

21 22 23 24 25 LSCC 10 9 8 7 6 5 4 3 2 1 ❖ First Edition

HELLO NINJA
Hello Stage fright

by N. D. Wilson   pictures by Forrest Dickison

HARPER
An Imprint of HarperCollinsPublishers

Making music is fun.

It is even more fun with friends!

Georgie shouts over the music,

"You're really good.

You should play at my

dance recital on Saturday."

"Will there be people there?" I ask.
Sometimes my tummy rumbles
when I perform in front of people.
I don't like the way that feels.

Georgie gives me a strange look.

"That's what a recital is for!"

"I am nervous," I tell her.

"What if I make a mistake?"

"I understand. Being on stage

can feel scary," Georgie says.

Georgie is so nice.

I don't want to let her down.

"Okay, Georgie. I'll give it a try!"

My tummy rumbles when I say that,

but I put on a brave face.

"Hooray!" Georgie says.

"Thank you, Wes."

"Let's practice!" I reply, getting excited.

"I have a song to learn!"

When recital day comes,

I am very nervous!

I can't keep this a secret.

"I'm scared, Georgie," I say.

"Oh no, Wesley," Georgie says.

"What are you afraid of?"

"What if I mess up?" I ask.

Georgie pats me on the back.

"Well, whenever I mess up,

I just smile and keep on going.

Want to try it?"

But I am too nervous to smile.

There are so many people out there!

Pretzel strikes a ninja pose.

"Good idea, Pretzel," Georgie says.

"Wesley, you can do this.

You just need to be a ninja!"

"Good idea!" I say.

Georgie pumps a fist in the air.

"Let's do this!"

We bow to each other.

"Hello, ninja," I say.

"Yes, hello," says Georgie.

We are ready for anything now!

This is strange!

The stage has turned

into a giant drum kit.

And the people are all

huge stone giants!

"What is this?" Georgie asks.

"At least they are all asleep," I say.

"They would be really scary awake."

Kuma!

"Ninjas!" Kuma says.
"An evil wizard
put these giants to sleep,
and now he is going to
make the volcano erupt."

A little stone girl

slides off Kuma's back.

"Please, ninjas!

Help my family," she says.

"Okay! Time to wake up some giants!"

The volcano is rumbling.

I can see lava and smoke!

"Be extra loud!" Georgie says.

"Even if we make mistakes!"

BOOM! BOOM! BOOM!

Georgie begins to dance
on the drum as hard as she can.
Pretzel is bouncing on the giant drum
like it is a trampoline!

I am going to drum the loudest
that I have ever drummed!

BOOM! BANG! CRASH! BOOM!

Oops. I broke my drumstick.

"Why did you stop?" Georgie asks me.

"We have to be loud

and fast and brave!"

"But I messed up.

I broke my drumstick," I say sadly.

"You still have one!" Georgie yells.

"You can do it!"

I cannot worry about my mistake.

I have to keep playing!

"We have to be the fastest ninjas ever,

or these statues will melt," I say.

"Georgie, can you dance

across the cymbals?"

Oh no!

The wizard turned my drumstick

into soft cotton candy.

What am I going to do now?

Pretzel is doing a great job,

and Georgie is too.

They are very loud!

But the giants are still asleep.

I should not stop!

I will use my hands and do my best!

BONG!

If I go my very fastest,

I can hit every drum

with my hands and feet.

But this is making me very dizzy!

"Faster!" the stone girl yells.

"The lava is coming!"

"This is as loud and as fast

as I can go!" Georgie shouts.

"Hey!" I say.

"We should try doing this

at the same time!"

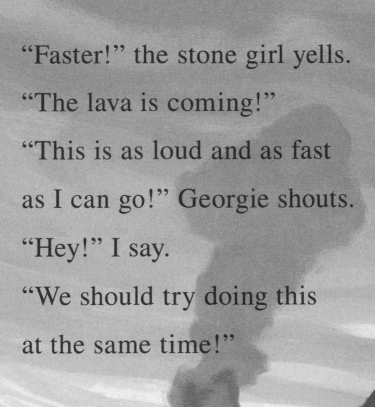

"Good idea!" Georgie says.

We jump together

on Pretzel's big drum.

We flip together

across the giant cymbals

and bounce off the drums

where I broke my stick.

We are much louder!

"It is working!" the stone girl yells.

"The statues are cracking!"

The stone giants

jump to their feet just in time.

They stand on their chairs,

clapping and cheering!

Everyone is looking at me,

and I am . . . smiling!

Everyone else is too.

Georgie and I make a great team!

And Pretzel is the best cat ever.

"I am so proud of you, Wesley,"

Georgie says later that day.

"Thanks, Georgie. I am too," I say.

Georgie claps her hands.

"Hey, since you shared

my recital with me,

I want to share something with you."

"Georgie, this is awesome!" I say.
"I know how much you love
secret forts—and this one
is super-duper secret,"
Georgie says with a wink.

Just like music, forts are more fun with friends!